Speak Up, Tommy!

To Miky and all the hard-working dogs
who help to keep us safe – J.D.G.

For Nate and Jack – D.M.

Text copyright © 2012 by Jacqueline Dembar Greene
Illustrations copyright © 2012 Lerner Publishing Group, Inc.

KAR-BEN PUBLISHING, INC.
A division of Lerner Publishing Group, Inc.
241 First Avenue North
Minneapolis, MN 55401 U.S.A.
1-800-4-Karben

Website address: www.karben.com

Library of Congress Cataloging-in-Publication Data

Greene, Jacqueline Dembar.
    Speak up, Tommy! / by Jacqueline Dembar Greene ; illustrated by Deborah Melmon.
        p.   cm.
    Summary: Tommy, who recently moved to America from Israel, is teased because he does not know English well and so does not speak loudly, but when a police officer visits Tommy's class with a police dog that only understands Hebrew, friendship blooms.
    ISBN: 978–0–7613–7497–8 (lib. bdg : alk. paper)
    [1. Immigrants—Fiction. 2. Language and languages—Fiction. 3. Police—Fiction.
4. Police dogs—Fiction. 5. Human-animal communication—Fiction. 6. Jews—United States—Fiction.] I. Melmon, Deborah, ill. II. Title.
PZ7.G834Sp 2012
[E]—dc23   2011029754

Manufactured in the United States of America

1 – BP – 7/15/12

Speak Up, Tommy!

Jacqueline Dembar Greene

Illustrated by
Deborah Melmon

KAR-BEN
PUBLISHING

Tommy stayed by himself at recess, tossing a tennis ball against the school building.

"Do you know how to play football?" Charlie asked. "We're going to throw some passes."

Tommy was puzzled. "A football isn't to throw," he said. "A football is to kick."

Charlie laughed. "That's soccer!" he exclaimed.

Tommy was confused. When he lived in Israel his football was round. You kicked it down the field into the goal. "I don't know this American football game," he mumbled.

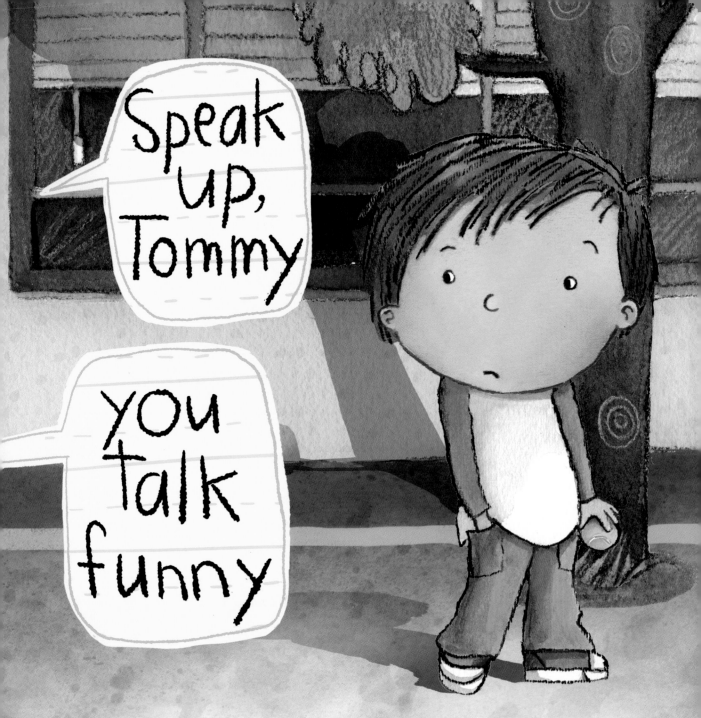

"Speak up, Tommy," teased Josh, imitating their teacher.

Charlie and Josh punched each other's arms and snickered. "You talk funny," said Charlie. Then they ran off.

Tommy's face grew hot. Why had he spoken English? The kids always teased him when he did. English words were hard to pronounce. In America, even his name had changed. In Israel his name was Tomer, which means "palm tree." He always stood taller when someone spoke his name. Now it was easier to be Tommy.

When it was time for reading circle, Tommy shrank down in his chair, trying to become invisible.

But Ms. Anderson called on him. "Would you begin, please, Tommy?"

There was nothing Tommy hated more than reading out loud, except having to read first. The words on the page swam in front of his eyes.

The 'r' sound rolled and trilled as he read. "Ron likes to run," he whispered. "Ron races along."

"Speak up, Tommy," said Ms. Anderson. "We can barely hear you." Some students giggled.

Ms. Anderson gave them a stern look. "Tommy's still learning English, and it's difficult at first. In this class we're a team, so let's cheer him on." She smiled at Tommy. "You're doing fine. But do speak up."

Tommy shook his head. He wouldn't speak English in school again.

After reading circle, Ms. Anderson gave Tommy a worksheet for tracing letters. They didn't look anything like Hebrew letters. He named each new letter in his head as he traced its shape. "A, B, C…" If only they looked more like *Aleph, Bet, and Gimel.*

"You're tracing letters?" Josh asked. "We did that in Kindergarten."

Tommy was glad when a knock on the door interrupted the teasing.

"As you know, we've been learning about our town," Ms. Anderson said, "and today we have special visitors from the Police Department."

The class had visited the Town Hall, the Post Office, and the Fire Station. Tommy liked field trips because he got to listen and didn't have to speak a word.

OUR TOWN

When Ms. Anderson opened the door, a man in a blue uniform walked in leading a frisky dog. "This is Officer Sweeney and his police dog Samson," she said.

Tommy's eyes opened wide. The Yellow Lab looked just like his dog Sabra who had to stay in Israel when his family moved. His grandparents were taking good care of her, but Tommy missed his dog every day.

"Sit," commanded Officer Sweeney. He pushed down on Samson's rump.

"When Samson was a puppy, he was chosen to become a special police dog," the officer explained. "He can smell things that people can't."

"My dog can smell a pizza box in a trash can," said Charlie.

Officer Sweeney grinned. "Not only can Samson smell food, but he's trained to smell things that could hurt people."

Tommy gasped. In Israel, police and dog teams helped to keep people safe. Samson must be one of those dogs!

"Police dogs work hard," said Officer Sweeney. "If Samson finds something suspicious, I reward him with a toy. He especially loves balls!"

Tommy fingered the tennis ball in his pocket, and suddenly Samson saw it and started to bark. Officer Sweeney whispered in the dog's ear, but Samson just gave him a puzzled look and kept barking. "Quiet!" said the officer.

QUIET!

Without warning, Samson pulled free and ran to Tommy, pawing at his pocket. The students laughed, and Tommy was glad that for once, they weren't laughing at him.

Ms. Anderson rang her bell for silence.

With all the commotion, Tommy forgot that he didn't want to speak English out loud. In fact, he forgot to speak English at all. He could only think in Hebrew.

"*Sheket!*" he blurted out. Instantly, Samson stopped barking. He looked expectantly at Tommy.

"That's it!" Officer Sweeney exclaimed. "That's the Hebrew word for 'quiet.' I've been trying to say that, but Samson doesn't understand me."

The students looked at the police dog sitting quietly at Tommy's feet.

"Where did you learn to speak Hebrew?" Officer Sweeney asked.

"I'm from Israel," Tommy explained. "I speak Hebrew lots better than English." Officer Sweeney didn't laugh. And this time Charlie and Josh didn't laugh, either.

Officer Sweeney scratched his head. "Samson was trained in Israel. I have a list of Hebrew commands, but when I try to say them, Samson ignores me." He chuckled. "And he doesn't understand a word of English!"

Ms. Anderson arched her eyebrows. "I think you need to practice your Hebrew," she said.

The officer put his arm around Tommy's shoulder. "We could be a team," he said. "If you help me speak Hebrew, I'll help you with English."

"Neat!" Charlie exclaimed. "Tommy's going to train a police dog!"

Josh looked interested. "Maybe you could teach us Hebrew, too," he added.

Tommy found his voice. "Sure," he said, "if you teach me to play American football."

"It's a deal," Josh agreed.

Tommy held up the tennis ball. *"Shev,"* he said to Samson. "Sit." The dog sat still as Tommy tossed the ball to Charlie. Then Charlie hid it inside his desk.

"*Tavi*," Tommy said. "Fetch." Samson trotted directly to the spot where the ball was hidden and brought it to Tommy. Tommy tossed it high in the air. "*Tafas!*" he commanded. "Catch!" The dog caught the ball in mid air and dropped it at Tommy's feet.

"*Kelev tov!*" he praised him. And then he spoke up loud and clear. "Good dog!"

Author's Note

Speak Up, Tommy! was inspired by a newspaper article about Sgt. John Fosket of the Helena, Montana Police Department, who was given a dog by an organization called Pups for Peace. The dog, Miky, was specially trained to sniff out hidden explosives and to sense someone acting suspiciously.

Sgt. Fosket had just one problem. Miky had been trained in Israel and only understood Hebrew commands.  The officer made himself flash cards with the Hebrew words, but had difficulty pronouncing them. Eventually, he enlisted the help of a Hasidic rabbi and a former member of the Israeli Defense Forces. Thanks to his Hebrew-speaking friends, the officer and the dog became a perfect team. They patrol the Montana Capitol building, and are sometimes called to investigate bomb threats.

English/Hebrew Dog Commands

Heel Ragli
Sit Shev
Stay He'asher
Down Artzah
Come Bo
Stand Amod

Fetch Tavi
Jump K'fotz
Go Out Hachutzah
Come Inside Kaness
Go Ahead Kadimah
Find Chapess
Guard Sh'mor
Let Go Azov
Eat Tochal
No Lo
Good Dog Kelev Tov
Quiet Sheket
Catch Tafas

Jacqueline Dembar Greene is the award-winning author of more than 30 books for young readers. Her books include the Rebecca Rubin series for American Girl, *The Secret Shofar of Barcelona,* and *Butchers and Bakers, Rabbis and Kings,* a finalist for the National Jewish Book Award. She lives in Wayland, Massachusetts.

Deborah Melmon has illustrated greeting cards, cookbooks, and children's books, as well as environmental art for the California Science Museum. She first realized she was going to be an artist when a paper-mache lion she created in seventh-grade art class was so large that it had to be driven home in the trunk of her parents' Oldsmobile with the lid up! Her previous books include *Picnic at Camp Shalom.* She graduated from the Academy of Art University in San Francisco and lives in Menlo Park, California with her dog.